Anonymous

The affecting story of the children in the wood

Anonymous

The affecting story of the children in the wood

ISBN/EAN: 9783337214630

Printed in Europe, USA, Canada, Australia, Japan

Cover: Foto ©Andreas Hilbeck / pixelio.de

More available books at **www.hansebooks.com**

QUARREL BETWEEN NED AND DICK.

THE
AFFECTING STORY
OF THE
CHILDREN IN THE WOOD.

PORTLAND:
S. H. COLESWORTHY:
1887.

THURSTON & CO., PRINTERS AND STEREOTYPERS,
No. 68 Exchange Street, Portland, Maine.

THE

CHILDREN IN THE WOOD.

———

A GOOD little boy whose name was Edgar, and his sister, whose name was Jane, were the children of a gentleman and lady who lived in Norfolk. Edgar and Jane were often told, that happiness depended on goodness; and that, to be good and happy, they must love each other, and never quarrel. Admired by every body for their dutiful behavior to their father and mother, and their affection for each other, they were still in their tender years when they had the misfortune of losing their kind parents.

Was not this a sad thing for little Edgar, and Jane? Indeed it was, and although very young, they were exceedingly grieved when their poor,

sick father and mother were dying. When together in the parlor, one morning, during their
parents' illness, while they were amusing themselves by viewing the pictures, one of the servants, with tears in his eyes, came and told them,

that their poor father and mother, who were dying,
had sent for them up stairs. They did not know
what dying meant; so they left the parlor, happy
to go to their kind parents.

The children on entering the room, ran to embrace them, and while they were proving the affection of their innocent hearts, they burst into tears, for they now saw their father and mother worse than ever; very pale and hardly able to speak. "My dear children," said the father in a feeble voice, "I sent for you to receive my last blessing, as it is the will of Almighty God that I should shortly leave you. He is the only giver of all good; pray to him night and morning for his protection. This, my dear children, I have often told you; but remember now, that I can never tell it you again."

His feeble voice was almost exhausted, but, pausing, he revived again, and added, "When I am in my grave, your uncle will take you home to his house; you must then obey him as you do me, and I hope you will always be good and happy." He was quite tired with this exertion, for he had but a few minutes longer to live. Tenderly embracing them again and again, he bade

them adieu, until they should meet in another
world. Scarcely had he uttered these words when
his weeping infants beheld him close his eyes in
death. This gentleman's brother, the children's
uncle, had come to visit him during his illness; he
recommended the children to his care, telling him
that he had no other friend on earth, and unless
that he was good to his boy and girl, they might
be greatly injured. "You must," said he, "be

father, mother, and uncle, all in one ; for I know not what will become of our dear children when we are dead and gone." Their mother then begged of him to be very kind to her sweet babes. " On you," said she, " dear brother, depends our children's happiness or misery, in this world, and God will reward you according as you act towards them." With many tears she bid Edgar and Jane farewell ; clasping them in her arms, and commending them to the protection of the Almighty, she reclined her head on the pillow, repeating, " God bless you, God bless you, my dear children !" After saying this she was never heard to speak again.

The uncle had promised his brother and sister, that he would do all they had asked of him ; but how faithfully he kept his promise, will be seen by and by. He lived in a fine house, surrounded with a large park, a great many miles distant ; so he ordered his servants to prepare the carriage, that he might take home these little orphans to

his elegant mansion.   In the meantime he opened
his brother's will, which made him the guardian of
the property left for Edgar and Jane.   Edgar was
to inherit three hundred pounds a year, when he
was of age ; and Jane's portion was five hundred
pounds in gold, to be given her on the day she
was married ; but in case they died while infants,
their uncle was to take possession of the whole
fortune.

All the neighbors were much grieved for the
death of this gentleman and lady.   The rich re-
gretted the loss of two worthy friends, whose so-
ciety was always pleasant and agreeable ; while
the poor lamented them, because that they were
deprived of kind and benevolent protectors.

The little orphans were still weeping, when their
uncle sent for them, and bid them cry no more.
They remembered their father's dying words,
which charged them to obey their uncle ; so they
wiped away their tears, though they remained
very dull for a long time afterwards.

The carriage was now ready to convey them to their uncle's seat, and with heavy hearts they left their native home.

After traveling about ten miles, they stopped at a small village for the coachman to refresh his horses. As Edgar and Jane were regretting the loss of their good parents, they had not been cheerful on their journey as usual, so their uncle determined to stay here about an hour, and strive to amuse them by walking about. It was a very pretty place, and being the residence of several wealthy families, was adorned with elegant houses, and grounds beautifully laid out. On alighting from the carriage, they inquired the name of this delightful village. It was the Vale of Content. The beauty and good order of it were really remarkable; and notwithstanding the number of poor cottages, there was not one beggar or idle person. Now, how do you think this happened? Because that the rich took care to assist the poor, and see that their children were well employed as soon as they were able to work; and this was the reason that the inhabitants were all happy, and that they called their residence the Vale of Content. A few years since, a large, commodious work-house was erected for the reception of those poor, whom age or illness rendered burdens to their families. Here were likewise received all the poor little boys and girls who had lost their parents; and these helpless orphans were supported and educated at the expense of the parish. Edgar and Jane were passing this building while the children were amusing themselves. Some were playing at trap and ball, some at marbles, whilst others were reading little story books,

which had been given them as a reward for their
diligence. At the sound of a bell, they all quit-
ed their amusements, and returned into the house,
to employ themselves in reading or writing, and
be instructed in those trades by which they were
to gain their livelihood in future. They were
now all assembled, and the spinning wheels and
weaving machines began to move so briskly, that
the noise surprised Edgar and Jane very much,
who stood peeping through the rails. One of the
overseers drew near the window to pull down the
sash, and observing the three strangers begged
them to walk in. Very willingly they accepted
the invitation, and ascending a few steps, entered
a long room, on one side of which were placed
the spinners, and on the other side the weavers.
The spinning consisted of wool, which was brought
here in large quantities at the time of sheep-
shearing. This store lasted all the winter, until
the returning season for collecting this useful com-
modity. Some were employed in picking and

combing it, while others, standing at wheels made on purpose for children, prepared it for weaving and knitting.

When spun it is called WORSTED, from a town in Norfolk, famous for woolen manufactures. The art of weaving was brought into England in the year 1331, and having been much practised ever since, is now arrived at very great perfection. The loom, and the machine by which the balls of worsted were wound into skeins, were considered very wonderful inventions by the travellers, who had never seen such a manufactory before. The spinners, the winders, and the weavers would have engaged their attention longer had they not been asked to visit other rooms, where reading, writing and knitting were going forward. All they saw amused them very much : but at last their uncle summoned them to leave this little seat of industry, and to return to the carriage ; for, he said, he was afraid they would scarcely reach his house before the close of the day. With that obedience which all good children show, even to a wish of a parent, they instantly complied, and, accompanied by their uncle, left this well ordered school of industry. In repassing the Vale of Content, Edgar and Jane again admired the beauty, the order, and the neatness that reigned there. But their uncle, who had no taste for the simple pleasures which appeared to favor the happiness of the people in this village, hastened the children on to the carriage. The coach drove fast, and

about seven o'clock in the evening, they reached an elegant, spacious mansion, placed in an exten-

sive park, which was well stocked with deer. Their
uncle now told them that this was his dwelling,
and that it was called Bashaw Castle. They all
alighted from the carriage; and the children
being wearied with their day's excursion, even
novelty lost, with them, all power of attraction,
and they immediately begged permission to go to
bed; so they wished their uncle good night, and
Betty, the house maid, lighted them up to their
chambers. Like good children, who had been
well instructed, they immediately knelt down and
said their prayers, for no fatigue could make them
forget this duty. But though so tired, instead of
falling asleep directly, as might have been expected, the stillness of the night, and the gloom which
to weak minds seems always attendant on darkness,
brought back to their minds the remembrance of
their loved parents, who were now, alas! lost to
them forever. Many a tear did they shed at this
recollection; but sleep at length overpowered
them; and in the morning they arose with the

lively, happy spirits of youth. They now descended hand in hand, walked about, and gazed at all the fine things they saw : they looked with astonishment at the spacious halls, the lofty chambers, the extensive flower gardens, and the fine hot-houses.

"How different is all this," said Edgar, " from my father's small house, his nice orchard, and pretty cornfields!"

JANE. "So it is, Edgar ; but I like home better, because papa and mamma were with us then, and they were so good and indulgent that we were always happy."

EDGAR. "Yes, sister, so we were. But I think my uncle must be very happy, too, with so many good things around him, and such a fine house."

Master Edgar little thought that his uncle, though thus surrounded with seeming plenty and luxury, was a stranger to all felicity ; for he was very wicked, and had therefore no internal comfort, in which consists the larger part of happiness.

He passed his days in idleness; he seldom read
his bible, or any other good book; nor did he at-
tend any place for divine worship, which might be
one reason why he continued so wicked. His
amusements even were barbarous; he was very
fond of cock-fighting, and such inhuman diver-
sions. Eating and drinking merely for the indul-
gence of appetite, was his great delight; and
he would pass half his days playing at cards.
Though he possessed a great deal of money, he
was so extravagant, and ordered so many more
things than he had money to pay for, that he felt
constantly the distress of poverty, and was un-
just, because he did not pay his debts.

And here, my young friends, I have with sorrow, placed before you the character of a very
wicked man, and shown you what conduct it was
that led him to the horrid crime of INTENDED
MURDER. You will, I am sure, turn from the pic-
ture with aversion: yet I wish you to dwell upon
it sufficiently to avoid similar faults yourselves.

Edgar and Jane, though very good children, still, like other very young persons, they required from time to time admonition from some wise friend. They had lost those tender parents that would have guided them to all good, and their uncle never heeded them; whether they done well or ill, he regarded it not. So Jane would

sometimes work, and sometimes would Edgar read to her out of the pretty little books his father had

formerly given them; but very often would they
throw aside the work and the books, and run in
the park all day with the deer. But these poor
little children had no one to remind them that it
was wrong to be idle, so they were not so much to
blame as those who act ill notwithstanding they
receive good counsel.

Their uncle's estate, from his negligence and
extravagance, was going quite to ruin. His land
was no longer fruitful, as formerly, because it
wanted proper culture ; and, in consequence of all
this, his income was considerably lessened. He
often meditated on some way in which he could
get money ; and, from his wicked deeds, having
lost the favor of the Almighty, and being no longer under the guidance of his grace, what wicked
thought do you think was permitted to enter his
head? The shocking one of murdering the pretty
little children, of whom he was guardian, that he
might possess their fortune. Now, instead of instantly repressing this horrid thought, he indulged

it, paused upon it, revolved it in his mind, and
at length determined to put in execution the barbarous suggestion of this dark moment. How

bad, how wicked may man become if forsaken by
an offended God! Mark this example of mortal
depravity. He was at first idle, extravagant, and
now he is ready to commit murder. He resolves
to do it; but to conceal his cruelty, he told his

wife and all his acquaintance that he would send his little nephew and niece to a relative of his in London, that they might be there educated.

The children were very happy in the expectation of this journey, for their uncle said they should go on horseback, and at the sight of the horses they rejoiced exceedingly. But this was only to deceive them, for he had hired two ruffians to commit the barbarous deed which he had contemplated. So these two frightful men took Edgar and Jane and seated them on the horses before them, and set off, at first, at a moderate speed, telling the children stories as they went along, which amused them very much, and their little innocent prattle in asking and answering questions, tended to soften the hearts of these two ruffians, named Ned and Dick, and they repented that they had engaged to murder them. Yet Dick said that he would do it, as he had been paid largely by their uncle. Ned had likewise received as much money, but he declared that he could not do this wicked deed.

Now they had traveled all day, and it was sun-
set when they entered a thick wood. They left
their horses at the entrance of the wood, and walked some distance through several narrow by-paths,
Ned and Dick quarrelling all the way; one was
for doing as they had agreed with the uncle, and
murder the poor babes; but the other would not,
so that at last they come to blows, and both fought

until Ned, who was the most powerful, killed his adversary. The fight made little Edgar and Jane tremble sadly, as they beheld the two men in deadly combat, and caused them to cry bitterly. When the battle was ended, Ned returned to the children, and bade them cry no more. Taking them by the hand, two long miles he led them on.

Poor babes! The ruffian now resolved to leave

them in the dismal forest, to perish with cold and hunger. They often asked him for food; at length he said he would fetch them some. So he left them, telling them to wait for his return; but it was not his intention to return. In vain did little Edgar and Jane wander up and down the thick wood to look for Ned.

At one time they sat down and repeated the following verses:

Why, O my soul, why thus deprest?
  And whence this anxious fear?
Let former favors fix thy trust,
  And check the rising tear.

When darkness, and when sorrows rose,
  And prest on every side,
Did not the Lord sustain thy steps?
  And was not God thy guide?

Affliction is a stormy deep,
  Where wave resounds to wave:
Tho' o'er my head the billows roll,
  I know the Lord can save.

Perhaps, before the morning dawns,
  He'll reinstate my peace:
For he who bade the tempest roar,
  Can bid the tempest cease.

In the dark watches of the night,
   I'll count his mercies o'er :
I'll praise him for ten thousand past,
   And humbly sue for more.

Then, O my soul, why thus deprest ?
   And whence this anxious fear ?
Let former favors fix thy trus
   And check the rising tear

Here will I rest, and build my hopes,
   Nor murmur at his rod ;
He's more than all the world to me,
   My health, my life, my God.

Arising from their mossy seat, they walked
again in search of Ned ; but, alas ! he was not to
be seen. In vain did they call upon him to come
and bring them food: Cruel creature ! he was

quite gone from the poor helpless babes. Hand
in hand, they wandered in the dismal forest, pick-
in black-berries from many a bush, to satisfy
keen hunger, till dark night drew on, and they
sunk exhausted on the cold ground.

They had not lain many minutes when an old
woman happened to pass that way. She was very
poor, and had been spinning all day to get a few

hard earned pence, and had come out in the dusk of evening to collect some sticks to make her fire. She saw these children: "What merciless wretch!" she exclaimed, " has left these little innocents thus to perish ? Whoever it is, their wicked purpose shall be defeated, for I will take them home, I will warm them by my fire, I will feed them with my supper."

Ye rich and ye affluent, who sometimes neglect to do good, take an example from this poor woman; see, though so poor, she can show pity, and perform a deed of charity.

As the old woman was passing along with the children, Ned, the ruffian passed them. He was returning into the wood to seek these babes, for though he had intended to let them remain to perish, he had not resolution to do so ; but when he saw they had found protection, he passed silently on, and the children being senseless, no one knew him. He determined, however, to stay two or three days in the neighboring village, that he might see what became of these poor little orphans, which he accordingly did. Now the good woman took them to her little cot; there she cherished them, warmed them, fed them, and being too poor to support them wholly herself, she got admittance for them into the School of Industry, which was in the village, near her. This school was supported by the bounty of all the wealthy families in the parish. Here little Edgar and Jane were taken good care of; they were well instructed, and taught to be very good and very industrious.— They were considered as very poor children, and so really they were now. Jane learned to read, to write, to work, to knit and to spin; and Edgar was taught to read, to write, and to be a gardener. One Sunday, a charity sermon was preached for the benefit of this school, and here is the pretty hymn which some of the children sang: —

HYMN.

To Thee, Almighty God and King,
　For thy parental care,
To Thee ten thousand thanks we bring,
　In homage, praise, and prayer ;
For friends and favor we rejoice,
　And ev'ry mercy giv'n ;
In grateful sounds we raise our voice,
　To thank the God of Heav'n.

The bounteous man, who spreads his store,
　Is favor'd in thy sight ;
Crown him with treasure ever more,
　And bless the widow's mite.
Our lot in life marked out by thee,
　With joy will we pursue ;
O, may we all thy goodness see,
　Each day thy praise renew.

Tho' poor in honor, poor in place,
　　O make us still thy own;
That, rich in virtue, rich in grace,
　　We may approach thy throne;
We sin in thought, in word, in deed,
　　Yet hope shall never cease
While our Redeemer's merits plead
　　For pardon and for peace.

The children at this school were taught to be
very good, and the masters and instructors took
so much care of them, that they were very happy.
Little Edgar and Jane remained here quite con-
cealed from all their former friends; and, as they
were supposed to be no longer inhabitants of this
world, their wicked uncle became possessor of all
their fortune; but as he acquired his riches un-
justly and cruelly, he could not enjoy them, for
his guilty conscience always tormented him. If
his friends came to visit him, he was not cheerful

enough to amuse them ; and at night, when he re-
tired to rest, he was afraid to close his eyes, for
then, frightful dreams presented themselves to his
imagination.   In his sleep, he thought he saw the
ruffians stabbing the two infants who had been left
under his care, while they, poor children, clung to
him for protection, which he inhumanly refused.
Sometimes he dreamed that the wrath of God
punished him for his wickedness, by depriving him
of all his wealth, his houses, his lands, and his
money, so that he was brought to extreme indi-
gence, and even implored his daily subsistence of
the passing crowd ; and that his children did not
exist to succor him in this wretched situation.   At
present this was only a dream, but soon, very soon,
he suffered in reality what his guilty conscience
had so often terrified him with, in sleep; and
though he now felt the displeasure of Almighty
God, he neither repented, nor even prayed for
forgiveness.   He possessed a great deal of land
that produced plentiful crops of corn and hay.—

3

Harvest was now just over, and his barns entirely
filled, for the season was remarkably fine and hot.
One night, during this sultry weather, the sky
darkened, and a dreadful storm arose.   Incessant-
ly the lightning flashed and the thunder rolled.—
As he could not sleep, he was walking about his
room very much agitated, when he beheld, with
terror and amazement, the fire from heaven fall
on the thatched roofs of his barns, and consume

in a few hours, the vast store he had collected
with so much anxiety.

Winter approached, and brought a severe frost, and as all his out houses, his corn, and his hay, were burned by the lightning, his cattle were now exposed, without food or shelter, to the inclemency of the season, so they all perished in the fields.

Having lost so much of his fortune, he was obliged to send his sons from home. A merchant in Portugal promised to employ them, and they

set sail with the hope of being his clerks. But the vessel had not yet left the coast of England, when

it struck on a fatal rock, and these unfortunate
boys perished on the wreck, amidst the dashing
waves.   When their wicked parent received the
news of their death, he gave himself up to despair;

and instead of being resigned to the punishment
inflicted by Heaven, and exerting himself as an
honest and prudent man would have done, to re-
trieve his fortune, he extravagantly spent the re-
mainder of his money.   His guilt, together with

the misfortune that had befallen him, as a punishment for his wickedness, prevented his settling in
any business, so continued idleness soon brought
him to the extreme of poverty. He mortgaged
his land, and when he had expended this sum for
his daily subsistence, he pawned his watch, and
some of the fine clothes he had worn when he was
a rich man. Now, that he had nothing more to
support himself he contracted still larger debts,
which he could never discharge; so his creditors
put him in prison, and here he ended his days
miserably, without a friend to comfort him or re-
lieve his distress. Thus it pleased Almighty God
that he should suffer! Wickedness, even in this
world, seldom goes unpunished, though goodness
does not always meet with its reward on earth.

The ruffian, Ned, who had left poor little Edgar and Jane in the forest, had generally lived
by plunder. He had robbed many a traveller of
his money, and pursued this course of life for a
long time undiscovered; but at length he was

brought to justice, and condemned to die for the
last robbery he had committed. Soon after his
sentence was pronounced, he confessed how wicked he had been, and that he had been hired to
murder poor little Edgar and Jane. He then re-
lated the circumstances of their journey, and that
he left them alone in the forest to perish; but that
some old woman had found them, and placed them
in a parish school. This account very much af-
fected the judge, and all who were present.

The ruffian, as he went to the gallows, appeared very penitent for all the bad actions of his past
life. He exhorted his companions, whom he was
leaving in prison, to avoid in future, if they were
acquitted, those crimes for which he acknowledged
that he was receiving a justly merited punishment.
After praying earnestly to be forgiven all his sins,
he ascended the scaffold, and soon entered on an
endless eternity.

The wicked uncle, who we before said was im-
prisoned for debt, and who died in his confinement,

having left no child to heir his encumbered estate, Edgar and Jane, whom the ruffian Ned had publicly, and with his dying breath declared were put into a parish school, were inquired for, found, brought forth into the world, and put in possession of BASHAW PARK, which soon changed its name for that of HAPPY DELL.   Here they long lived in uninterrupted peace.   The rich loved them for their goodness and courteousness, the poor blessed them for their charity and kindness; and the poor old woman who had formerly placed them in the School of Industry, they took home, and repaid the service she had done them, by shewing her unremitting kind attentions to the last day of her life.

Industry is the best security from vice, for those who are idle always meet with bad companions; be diligent, then, and you will rarely be tempted to do wrong.   Honesty is likewise the best policy; be just, therefore, to all, for it is virtue alone will

make you beloved, esteemed, and truly respected
through life.

And now, my little readers, having made these
reflections, and I hope, impressed upon your
minds the truth of them, by the foregoing history,
I will only detain you while I repeat a pretty
hymn, which was given to Edgar and Jane in the
School of Industry. They were one day rather
unhappy; they were thinking of their good father and mother whom they had lost, and of their
uncle's fine house, and of the pleasant walks which
they used to have in his park amongst the deer,
and these recollections made them shed some sor-
rowful tears. One of their masters observed their
affliction, and kindly gave them this pretty hymn,
which contains comfort for earthly grief, by di-
recting our hopes to eternal joys. Now here it is:

HYMN.

Eternal Ruler ! Mighty Power !
Thou God of peace in sorrow's hour,
When e'er the heart affliction knows,
From Thee unceasing comfort flows.

Supremely good ! then let us pray,
The God who gives and takes away,
To make us own Him just and wise,
When earthly blessings He denies.

No longer, then, let transient joy,
Our thoughts and fondest hopes employ,
But teach our hearts Thy will divine,
That bids us earth for Heaven resign.

And when our clay resigns its breath,
And falls to dust in silent death,
May the blest spirit soar above,
To praise the God of peace and love.

Edgar and Jane learned this pretty hymn, and often repeated it, as I hope you will all do; and and when raised to prosperity, greater than that which they had ever expected, they still remembered that earthly joys were uncertain, and they directed their hopes and wishes to that world where bliss is lasting and eternal.

CONCLUSION.

As we have now recited every particular which relates to THE CHILDREN IN THE WOOD, we shall offer a few considerations for the perusal of our young friends.

As you must feel the utmost hatred for the conduct of the unnatural uncle, it greatly concerns you to guard against the passions of avarice and ambition, which are two of the most detestable crimes that can pollute the human heart, or debase the character of a reasonable being. Whenever you give way to the dazzling and deceitful pleasures of pomp and greatness, then it is that you violate the dictates of conscience, and treasure up a baneful source of misery and wretchedness.

But when you presume to offend your Maker in a
still more daring degree, and proceed to commit
acts of cruelty, revenge, and even MURDER itself;
when you calmly and deliberately perpetrate the
most horrid deeds, and gratify the most licentious
appetites, how much you dread the all-searching
eye of that Being who can bring to light the hid-
den things of darkness. Remember, that what-
ever you say or do, even in the most secret place
or manner, it is all known to God, who knows the
secrets of all hearts! Let this important thought
have due weight with you, so that your conduct
at all times may be influenced by it, and then you
will reap the advantage of it, both here and here-
after. All your worldly transactions will prosper,
and your eternal state will amply reward you for
your cheerful obedience to the laws of Him who
made you.

A tale well known to those of old,
In many a winter's night been told;
While gaping children round appear,
And drop the sympathising tear.

When the dread tale was understood,
Of children starving in the wood,
Our grandsires each have wept ere now,
Our grandsires and our grandmas too.

And shall to ages yet unborn,
Who read the tale of these forlorn,
Still cause the tender tear to flow,
And melt the heart with others' woe.

A cruel uncle, wicked hate,
With all the terrors of his fate,
Shall strike a moral in the breast,
And make us cruelty detest.

Let every boy and girl be good,
And read THE CHILDREN IN THE WOOD.

INTRODUCTION TO THE BALLAD

No apology can be necessary for producing a reprint of so popular a ballad as "The Children in the Wood," the interest of which is destined to endure as long as pity itself, in the human, or in the Red-breast. In putting " these pretty babes" into fresh leaves, and helping to prevent such Flowers of the Forest from fading away, the Proprietor feels sure that he is doing a service to other "children young," by perpetuating a portion of that wholesome romance, which, like the bloom on the grape, clings with such loveliness and kindliness to the head and heart of youth. If the lover of art, in addition to the lover of nature, should derive a gratification from the reprint, through the character of the illustrations which accompany it, the highest aim will be answered—

that of decking so fair a pall " with scutcheons
meet and true, and handsome effigies."

The admirable Elia, in his Essays, makes men-
tion of an old mansion-house in Norfolk, tradition-
ally reported to have been the residence of the
" cruel uncle ;" and that, on a mantel, the whole
story was carved in oak, " down to the Robin
Red-breasts." This precious relic was afterwards
removed by some " foolish rich person," to give
place to one of more modern marble, of course,
made " thick and slab ; " and certainly the inno-
vator deserved a souse, with his new shelf, into
the Witches' Cauldron. Whether "the whole
story, down to the Robin Red-breasts," cut in box,
be worthy of a better fate, is now respectfully
submitted. It appears, by the name, as if the
story were destined to be perpetuated in its present form,— and that it could never be perfectly
told, until the Babes were shown, as Mr. Harvey has
shown them, to be the real Children in the Wood.

A

FAVORITE BALLAD.

Now ponder well, ye parents dear,
  These words which I shall write;
A doleful story you shall hear,
  In time brought forth to light.

A gentleman of good account,
  In Norfolk dwelt of late,
Who did in honor far surmount
  Most men of his estate.

Sore sick he was, and like to die,
  No help his life could save;
His wife by him as sick did lie,
  And both possessed one grave.

No love between these two was lost,
  Each was to other kind;
In love they lived, in love they died,
  And left two babes behind.

The one a fine and pretty boy,
  Not passing three years old;
The other, a girl, more young than he,
  And framed in beauty's mould.

The father left his little son,
  As plainly doth appear,
When he to perfect age should come,
  Three hundred pounds a year.

And to his little daughter Jane,
  Five hundred pounds in gold,
To be paid down on marriage-day,
  Which might not be controlled.

But if the children chance to die,
  Ere they to age should come,
Their uncle should possess their wealth,
  For so the will did run.

" Now, brother," said the dying man,
    " Look to my children dear ;
Be good unto my boy and girl,
    No friends else have they here :

" To God and you I recommend
    My children dear this day,
But little while be sure we have
    Within this world to stay.

You must be father and mother both,
    And uncle all in one ;
God knows what will become of them,
    When I am dead and gone."

With that bespake their mother dear:
  " O, brother kind," quoth she,
" You are the man must bring our babes
  To wealth or misery.

"And if you keep them carefully,
  Then God will you reward;
But if you otherwise should deal,
  God will your deeds regard."

With lips as cold as any stone,
  They kiss'd their children small;
"God bless you both, my children dear;"
  With that the tears did fall.

These speeches then their brother spake,
    To this sick couple there:
" The keeping of your children small,
    Sweet sister, do not fear;

" God never prosper me nor mine,
    Nor aught else that I have,
If I do wrong your children dear,
    When you are laid in grave."

The parents being dead and gone,
    The children home he takes,
And brings them straight unto his house,
    Where much of them he makes.

He had not kept these pretty babes
A twelve-month and a day,
But, for their wealth, he did devise
To make them both away.

He bargained with two ruffians strong,
Which were of furious mood,
That they should take these children young,
And slay them in a wood:

And told his wife and all he had,
He did the children send
To be brought up in fair London,
With one that was his friend.

Away then went these pretty babes,
    Rejoicing at that tide,
Rejoicing with a merry mind,
    They should on cock-horse ride.

They prate and prattle pleasantly,
    As they rode on the way,
To those that should their butchers be,
    And work their lives decay.

So that the pretty speech they had
    Made murther's heart relent,
And they that undertook the deed,
    Full sore did now repent.

Yet one of them, more hard of heart,
    Did vow to do his charge,
Because the wretch that hired him,
    Had paid him very large.

The other won't agree thereto;
    So here they fell to strife,
With one another they did fight,
    About the children's life :

And he that was of mildest mood,
    Did slay the other there,
Within an unfrequented wood,
    While babes did quake for fear.

He took the children by the hand,
   Tears standing in their eye,
And bade them straightway follow him,
   And look they did not cry:

And two long miles he led them on,
   While they for bread complain;
" Stay here," quoth he, " I'll bring you some,
   When I come back again."

These pretty babes, with hand in hand,
   Went wandering up and down;
But never more could see the man
   Approaching from the town.

Their pretty lips with black-berries
  Were all besmeared and dyed,
And when they saw the darksome night,
  They sat them down and cried.

Thus wandered these two little babes,
  Till death did end their grief,
In one another's arms they died,
  As babes wanting relief:

No burial this pretty pair
  Of any man receives,
'Till Robin-red-breast painfully,
  Did cover them with leaves.

And now the heavy wrath of God
  Upon their uncle fell ;
Yea, fearful fiends did haunt his house,
  His conscience felt an hell:

His barns were fired, his goods consumed,
  His lands were barren made,
His cattle died within the field,
  And nothing with him stayed.

And in a voyage to Portugal,
  Two of his sons did die ;
And to conclude, himself was brought
  To want and misery.

He pawned and mortgaged all his land,
  Ere seven years came about;
And now at length this wicked act
  Did by this means come out:

The fellow that did take in hand,
  These children for to kill,
Was for a robbery judged to die,
  (Such was God's blessed will;)

Who did confess the very truth,
  As here hath been displayed:
Their uncle having died in jail,
  Where he for debt was laid.

You that executors be made,
　　And overseers eke,
Of children that be fatherless,
　　And infants mild and meek;

Take you example by this thing,
　　And yield to each his right,
Lest God with such like misery,
　　Your wicked minds requite.

THE END.